THE SLOPPY COPY SLIPUP

DyAnne DiSalvo

Holiday House / New York

Acknowledgments:

I would like to thank Ms. Roxanne Adonolfi and the faculty and students
from Joyce Kilmer Elementary School and Stockton Elementary School;
Ms. Harriet Fromme; my son, John Ryan; Adrianne Kalfopoulou; the band
Smash Palace; and my husband, Stephen Butler, for all their exuberant
support and outstanding inspiration.

Library of Congress Cataloging-in-Publication Data

DiSalvo, DyAnne.
The sloppy copy slipup / by DyAnne DiSalvo.—1st ed.
p. cm.
Summary: Fourth-grader Brian Higman worries about how his teacher Miss
Fromme—nicknamed The General—will react when he fails to hand in a writing
assignment, but he ends up being able to tell his story, after all.
ISBN 0-8234-1947-9
[1. Storytelling—Fiction.   2. Authorship—Fiction.   3. Schools—Fiction.
4. Humorous stories.]   I. Title.

PZ7.D6224Slo 2005
[Fic]—dc22
2004060777

ISBN-13: 978-0-8234-1947-0
ISBN-10: 0-8234-1947-9

For my charming
and lovely nieces,
    madeleine and Rachel

BIG HIG'S DISASTROUS NEWSLETTER

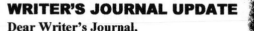
as keyboarded on my computer by Brian Higman

WRITER'S JOURNAL UPDATE

Dear Writer's Journal,
  Today I do not have my homework
and I am about to get another zero.
  Yours truly,
  Guess who?

←my mother

BRIAN HIGMAN'S MOTHER FINALLY HITS CEILING!

Really nice kid banished to Siberia for LIFE.
See more inside.

A PERSON WHO CAN MAKE A BIG DEAL OUT OF ANYTHING

Ana is the kind of person who can make a big deal out of anything. Last week when Martin Adaji put a tomato in his fruit painting, Ana made one of her big deals about whether a tomato was a fruit or a vegetable. I was glad when Mrs. Chila said that a tomato could be considered as both. It was a fruit that was used as a vegetable. In the plant group it was actually considered to be a berry.

← TOMATO

AHHHH

TRY THIS NEW RECIPE!

SLOW-ROASTED SURPRISE
Mix one big kid,
one late homework.
Add one angry teacher.
Turn on heat.
Stand back.
Expect anything!

QUOTE OF THE DAY FROM MR. MEYERS AT THE MUSIC STORE:

"Stevie, you send my blood pressure right through the roof."

artwork done by the outstanding Big Hig

WANTED: DEAD OR ALIVE
Brian Higman
Alias Big Hig
REWARD

EXTRA!
Brian Higman sets universal record for most detentions in world history.

BIG HIG'S CLASSROOM WEATHER REPORT:
Will the hurricane hit? Stay tuned for more DISASTROUS NEWS.

BIG HIG HOROSCOPE:
Caution! Planets are crisscrossing. This is NOT your lucky day.

POSITION WANTED:
Experienced person needed to help dig kid out of deep trouble. Send all inquiries to Hig.

This is not a good joke sorry ←

OUTSTANDING JOKE:
Question: Why did the centipede cross the road?
Answer: To get to the other side.

SOLVE ALL YOUR PROBLEMS AND WRITE TO MANNERS MATTER:

Dear Manners Matter,
Do you think it is bad manners for a teacher to fail an unfortunate yet outstanding student without listening to his whole reason first?
Yours truly,
A really nice kid

Dear A Really Nice Kid,
It would be very bad manners, indeed.
Sincerely,
Manners Matter

DESPERATE:
Soon-to-be great guitar player seeks bass player who feels the same. Must like rock and roll. SEND PHOTO!

more news coming soon...

contents

Chapter One
An Outstanding Zero

It was Monday morning. The entire kindergarten through fifth-grade classes at Franklin Elementary had just sat down after reciting the Pledge of Allegiance.

I, Big Hig, was fielding through my backpack, pretending to search for the written assignment I knew I didn't have.

"The word of the day is *outstanding*," my ex-best friend, Ana Newburg, announced over the loudspeaker. Why is Ana my ex-best friend? That's a whole other story I'll get to later.

"O-u-t-s-t-a-n-d-i-n-g." Ana spelled the word slowly. "It is an adjective meaning exceptional or terrific. For lunch we will be having *outstanding* macaroni and cheese with *outstanding* fresh fruit and your choice of *outstanding* juice or milk. Thank you. Have an *outstanding* day."

Ana held her mouth too close to the microphone and made the loudspeaker screech. "AHHHHH!" Robby Zao fell against his desk and covered his ears. Josh Mendez closed his eyes and made a sour face. I was grateful for any distraction. It was only a matter of time before my teacher, Miss Fromme, began to collect Monday morning's assignment—the first draft—better known to her class as *the sloppy copy.*

After we hand in our sloppy copy it comes back with a mess of corrections and suggestions from Miss Fromme. Like: *Brian, more description for this opening sentence, please.* Or: *Brian, please remember to use your five senses when you write.* Uh! The next rewrite checks for grammar and spelling. *Brian, you do not need all these commas, thank you.* Which finally brings us to the final copy, if we end up living that long.

I personally do not mind writing. The problem is that I never have anything exciting to write about. Thinking up an idea is the hardest part for me. Anything I ever think about writing is either too long, too short, or too boring.

For example, why do the kids call me Big Hig? Simple. I am the biggest kid in our class and my name is Brian Higman. End of story.

And how about my family? Well, let's see. I have a mother named Florence. My pop's name is George. My older brother is Denny. My younger brother is Stevie. And I have a dog named Patches.

I guess I could try to write something about them. But that's where the long and boring part comes in.

Once I tried to write about a fishing trip we all went on. It was the day my pop decided we needed to spend some family time together. The sun was shining like pizza. My mother got two fishing poles from the basement and sponged off the cobwebs. Denny and I wrapped five peanut butter and jelly sandwiches in tinfoil. Stevie was in charge of packing the snacks. Pop piled everything, including us, into our Subaru station wagon and off we went. Mom turned up the radio while Denny played an air guitar in the backseat. Stevie counted and re-counted the number of cookies he had in his bag. "One plus two is three. Three plus one is four." I was relieved to know that my little brother did not have any ideas to supply us with any of his so-called entertainment.

When we got to the lake, we unpacked our stuff into the little boat we rented. Well no sooner did Pop finally ripple our canoe to what promised to be a good spot for fishing, when Stevie began to feel sorry for the minnows we were about to use for live bait. He patted his life jacket. "Don't worry, fishies," Stevie said in his superhero voice, "I'll save you." Then he picked up the pail of minnows and emptied the entire bucket into the water, yelling, "Free the fishies! Free the fishies!" You can believe me or not, but this really happened. Who wants to hear a story like that? I didn't think it was very good.

So instead of handing it in to Miss Fromme, I gave her a blank piece of paper. That was the first time I got a red zero.

Miss Fromme says that it is good practice to be aware of the ordinary things that happen in your life and learn to write them down.

Dear Writer's Journal,
   Today I do not have my homework again and I am about to get another zero.
                Yours truly,
                guess who?

I was busy thinking of unexciting and ordinary things like journal writing and family fishing trips, when Miss Fromme motioned for the first table to stand. She pressed her lips together in a line. My stomach did a quick flip.

"First table," Miss Fromme said. "Ladies and Gentlemen! Less talk and more attention. This way, please." The kids at the first table made one messy line toward the front of the room. I watched as a pile of written assignments began to stack up on Miss Fromme's desk.

I could tell right away that Miss Fromme was not in a good mood. She did not even say thank you whenever another paper was added to the bunch. "Next table, please," said Miss Fromme.

I swallowed too much air at once and let out a little burp. It was all over for me. One more table and I'd be up there, too.

Ana Newburg walked into the classroom. She was all whoop-de-do from her loudspeaker announcement. She shook her bangs and rushed to her seat where she pulled out her sloppy copy. Ana held it up as if Miss Fromme had already given her an A+.

"Big deal," Robby Zao whispered to her from table three. He chomped on his pencil like a rabbit.

I opened my journal and wrote:

Ana is the kind of person who can make a big deal out of anything. Last week in art class, when Martin Adaji put a tomato in his fruit painting, Ana made one of her "big deals" about whether a tomato was a fruit or a vegetable. I was glad when Mrs. Chila said that a tomato could be considered as both. It was a fruit that was used as a vegetable. In the plant group it was actually considered to be a berry.

I put my pencil down.

Right now, the last thing I needed was for Ana Newburg to make some kind of big deal about me. After all, I had a very good reason for not having my written assignment. In fact, I had planned to do it all weekend. Only my weekend did not work out as I had planned. Now all I had to do was convince Miss Fromme to give me another chance.

Chapter Two
Don't Mess with the Facts

I sat in my seat and waited for my table to be called. I stared at my blank piece of paper. I could almost imagine the way it would look with the words written neatly on the page. It would have been chock-full of information—just like a newspaper.

The one thing I did know about was newspapers. Besides being the top salesperson at Robins Appliance Store, my pop was also the founder and publisher of *The Franklin Newsletter*.

The Franklin, as it is commonly known in our house, is the town's monthly newsletter. It keeps Franklin neighbors up-to-date on block parties, leaf cleanups, town meetings, horoscopes, weather reports, and other bits of local news that fill up a two-page leaflet. Don't Mess with the Facts is Pop's running motto.

My brother Denny says he's heard Pop recite his motto so many times that he doesn't even hear it anymore. Personally, I think Denny's bad hearing has less to do with my pop's motto and more to do with the so-called entertainment my little brother, Stevie, provides during the course of the day.

"Stevie, you send my blood pressure right through the roof."

I wrote that in my journal, too. That's a direct quote from Mr. Myers who owns the music store in town. And that goes double for me.

"Next table, please," Miss Fromme said. "The rest of the class please open your writers' notebooks and begin to journal your morning."

This is it, I told myself. I stood up. A long, loud bell rang. We were having an *outstanding* fire drill.

"Line leader up front, quickly," Miss Fromme said. "Quickly, quickly. Class, no talking or there will be no recess."

Kala Patel rushed to her position.

Saved by the bell! I love fire drills.

I stepped in line with the rest of my class and followed Kala into the great outdoors. We all went silently down the stairs and out to the back of the school yard.

"How come I never get to be the line leader?" Josh Mendez whispered to me. Josh had both hands stuck inside the pockets of his denim jacket. His glasses were crooked, and he smelled like lemon-scented laundry detergent.

"You were the line leader last month," I whispered back.

"I forgot," said Josh.

"I'm going to report you," Kala warned us.

The last thing I needed was for any more trouble. The autumn day was crisp and breezy. The trees looked like they were waving hello. I blew out a sigh of re-lief. At least in the school yard, I was tem-porarily saved. I relaxed a little and began to enjoy it. My mind took a break and started to wander.

Did I happen to mention that I am in the market to buy my first guitar? Well, I am. I've had my eye on a really cool electric guitar that has been in Mr. Myers's music store for about two weeks. It's second-hand, but it's as good as new. Whenever I am in there, which is usually a lot, Mr. Myers lets me check it out.

I always go out of my way never to touch anything or ask Mr. Myers too many questions while I'm in there. Mr. Myers is the nervous type. And my little brother, Stevie, makes him nervous. Mostly I try to go into the music store by myself, but usually I am keeping an eye on Stevie for my mother.

Stevie touches everything and asks about a million questions at the same time. He also insists on singing one of his so-called entertainment songs as he whizzes up and down the aisles.

"Phone, phone on the range," Stevie sings. "Excuse me, Mr. Myers, what kind of instrument is this? Does it come in green? Green is my favorite color. What's yours? Can I try out these drums?"

"Settle down, Stevie," I say just like Pop tells him.

But Stevie doesn't listen to me.

When I told Denny about the guitar I was going to buy, he said, "You mean the red-and-black Stratocaster that's in the window?"

At the time I was helping him tape up a rock-and-roll poster of this jamming new band called The Edge. Denny's room had sheet music and CDs stacked in neat rows along the fringe of his rug. He was the rhythm guitar player in his band, Questions No Answers, which, by the way, practiced every Saturday after-noon in the basement of my house.

Denny stepped back and looked at his poster.

"I think that's the same guitar that Harry wants to buy," he said.

Harry Harrington, the *neighborhood-famous* lead guitar player in Denny's band? The one who was also in his first year of high school just like Denny?

"He can't buy it!" I said. "That's the guitar I've been saving up for."

Denny shrugged. He tightened the little rubber band on the ponytail he had just started to grow.

"Talk to Harry about it," he said. "Maybe you can work something out."

Talk to Harry? "No way," I told him.

And that's when I decided to go to Myers's Music first thing Saturday morning to buy it.

I stamped my sneakers on the school-yard ground as I thought about what happened next. No wonder I didn't have the time to write my sloppy copy. The whole weekend was one big family emergency. I had a perfectly solid reason for not getting around to writing it.

"How much longer do we have to be out standing in this *outstanding* school yard?" Robby Zao said, resting his chin on my shoulder. "There isn't even a fire."

Robby was right. There was no fire. Except for the one that was burning inside my brain. The bad news was that we would not be in this

outstanding school yard forever. Sooner or later we were going back inside, and I'd have to face Miss Fromme.

"All *outstanding* students return to class," Mr. Zifferman, the principal, said through his megaphone.

Miss Fromme raised her hand in a motion for her class to follow. The one thought that kept following me around was Stevie. Stevie who follows me into my room whenever I want to be alone. Stevie who tries to follow me on his Big Wheel whenever I take a bike ride. Stevie who wants to do everything that I do and then tells my mother all about it.

"Guess what, Flo?" Stevie says. "Brian took me to the music store again."

That really gets me boiling. Stevie chums up to my mother like there's no tomorrow. He even calls her Flo, which is short for Florence, and my mother allows it.

"After all, he *is* the baby of the family," my mother says.

"Baby my foot," I say. Stevie is nearly five years old and he's never even been to school.

One day Stevie asked Flo if he could stay at home with her instead of going to kindergarten.

And just like that, my mother said yes. I mean, nobody ever told me that I didn't have to go to school.

"Stevie will learn at home," my mother says. "He'll be all set by the time first grade rolls around."

Right. But who has to mind Stevie when my mother needs help? Me. And guess who'd rather be minding a bunch of monkeys on a desert island, lost forever somewhere in the middle of the Pacific Ocean, instead of watching Stevie? Me.

The more I thought about Stevie the angrier I got. Here I was, with my life in my hands, and it was all Stevie's fault. If it weren't for Stevie, I would have had my sloppy copy already written and ready to hand in to Miss Fromme just like everybody else.

Back in the classroom Miss Fromme had settled into her seat like a war pilot ready for takeoff. She hunched her back and held on to her desk. The kids at my table took one look at her and stood up without being asked. I shuffled my feet from side to side. I could already imagine the writing on my tombstone:

Brian Higman
Nice Kid
Better Luck
Next time

Maybe one day the fact would be that I would take over *The Franklin* and write my head off. But here were the facts today:

Number one: Miss Fromme was waiting for me to give her my written assignment.

Number two: I didn't have it.

Number three: I would not be seeing the light of day for the rest of the week if I didn't say something fast.

Chapter Three
Face-to-Face with General Fromme

I stepped up to Miss Fromme's desk to give her my blank piece of paper. Well, it wasn't a completely blank piece of paper. I had already written my name on top. That should count for something.

The closer I got, the braver I became. I'd tell Miss Fromme exactly what happened. At first she would probably get a little angry, but then she would probably understand. She'd probably give me a little extra homework. And I'd probably do the same thing if I was her.

I smiled to myself. Everything would be fine.

So I did what any kid like me would do—I ran for the bathroom pass. I slipped my paper onto Miss Fromme's desk before it was even my turn.

I knew it was a dumb excuse to leave the room in such a hurry, but I needed more time to think. As I walked down the hall, I thought about Ana. Didn't I have enough problems already?

It never really bothered me that Ana was a girl. Our parents were friends, and we got along. I liked baseball. She liked baseball. I had a dog. She had a dog. We both liked rock and roll.

Then all of a sudden, things started to change. Ana didn't want to play baseball anymore. Me neither. We wanted to start a band instead. We bugged Denny to teach us how to play the guitar. Ana wanted to learn the bass. Robby Zao was taking drum lessons. Josh Mendez said he wanted to sing. Everything was going great.

But then Ana joined the orchestra. She took up the cello. Nadine Ali became her new best friend. Ana didn't come over on Saturdays anymore when Denny's band practiced.

"You can't just quit the band," I told her.

"What band?" said Ana. "You don't even have a guitar yet."

This was true. I didn't have a guitar yet. But all that was about to change. In the meantime maybe I will just put a personal ad in *The Franklin*:

Desperate:
   Soon-to-be great guitar player seeks bass player who feels the same.
   Must like rock and roll.
    SEND PHOTO!

On the way back from the bathroom, I could hear Miss Fromme reciting one of her favorite mottos: "Write about what you know. Or research what you don't."

I slinked into the classroom and put the bathroom pass back on the hook.

"Excuse me, Mr. Higman," Miss Fromme said. "You left me a piece of paper with your name written on it."

Miss Fromme folded her arms.

She tapped her foot like she was in a hurry.

"Miss Fromme," I said. "I can explain."

"This is not the first time, Mr. Higman," she said.

Miss Fromme was right. It was the second time.

I knew that if I came home with another zero in English, I would be seeing a lot more than red on my mother's face. I think you'd call it fury. My mother didn't fool around with things like this. The last time she grounded me I had no TV or PlayStation for a week. This time could only be worse.

The newspaper headline would read:

BRIAN HiGMAN'S Mother
finally HiTS CeiLiNG
Really nice kid banished to
SiBeRiA for LIFE.

Miss Fromme lifted her reading glasses as if a cloud of smoke had just fogged her lenses. She stared at me with her red marker ready on top of my blank piece of paper. Well, not totally blank.

I was cooked ... No! Baked. ... No! Burnt to a crisp. I could see it in *The Franklin:*

Try This New Recipe!
Slow Roasted Surprise
Mix one big kid,
One late homework,
Add one angry teacher.
Turn on heat.
Stand back.
Expect anything!

"It was all my little brother's fault," I blurted out.

Miss Fromme narrowed her eyes.

Miss Fromme. Just the name gives me the same chill as fingernails on a blackboard. In my family her name comes with a reputation.

The only wish that Denny ever had for me was, "I hope you don't get 'The General.'"

"The General," as Miss Fromme was respectfully known throughout the entire Franklin Elementary School, was not a teacher to mess with.

"Don't let her fool you when she folds her hands and tilts her head," Denny warned me early on. "That mean's she's setting the trap."

Miss Fromme folded her hands and tilted her head.

"Go ahead, Brian," she said to me. "You have my full attention."

"Thank you, Miss Fromme," I said, nearly saluting her.

I raised my chin and began to tell her what had happened.

"It was Saturday. I was all set for the beginning of a great weekend. I planned to do my

homework after lunch, and I had the whole morning to myself.

"I looked over at the bed next to mine. Stevie was still asleep. He had all the sheets bunched up to his neck. Our dog, Patches, was snoring on a pillow next to him. Stevie and Patches—now that was a match! We were never allowed to have a dog in our house until the day that Patches arrived. And I do mean *arrived*, which by the way is another whole other story.

"One afternoon I was in the living room drawing these really cool planes with a new felt-tipped pen I got. My mother was nearby on her piano, trying to figure out a song she wanted to learn. It was raining outside like you wouldn't believe, when all of a sudden there was this sound.

" 'Hooooooooow.'

"It was the kind of sound you couldn't put your finger on.

" 'Stop your howling,' Pop said to Stevie. 'A man can't work with a noise like that.'

"Stevie looked out from under the kitchen table. He was counting the collection of ba-nana stickers he had stuck underneath.

" 'That's not me, Pop,' Stevie said.

" 'Hooooow wow!'

"The noise was beginning to bug me, too.

"My mother pushed aside her piano bench and wove a pencil through her hair.

" 'That noise must be coming from the washing machine,' she said. 'I think it's time for a new one.' My mother went to check the washer, but it was spinning fine.

"Meanwhile, I could hear my brother Denny in the basement singing through his microphone. It sounded more like an 'ooooooo' than a 'hoooow wow!' Shaver banged his crash cymbal and kick-drum pedal while the crystals on our chandelier shook each time Ace Randall hit a bass note. 'Twang, Twang, EEEEEEEEEE.' The neighborhood-famous Harry Harrington raised the volume on his electric guitar.

" 'Hooooow wow! Wooooooooooo! Yoooow!' The noise was getting out of hand. I decided it was time to investigate."

I leaned against the white board and noticed that Miss Fromme was beginning to tilt her head the other way.

"And remember," I heard my brother's voice telling me. "If Miss Fromme tilts her head the other way, it means you need to use more descriptive language."

"So I got up from my soft, comfortable green couch with the red-and-gold flowered pillows and decided it was time to investigate," I said it again only this time better. **"The annoying sound was coming from somewhere. It made the lamp shade shake like jelly."** Hey! I thought. That simile was good.

Miss Fromme listened. She did not look impressed.

ALERT! RED ZERO CLOSING
in ON ALL SIDES.
RUN FOR YOUR LIFE
iF YOU CAN!

Chapter Four
Fleas Not Lice

Position Wanted:
Experienced person needed to help dig kid out of deep trouble.

That's how the classified ad in The Franklin *was going to read when I got around to writing it.*

"Sorry, Miss Fromme," I said, trying not to lose my train of thought. "I think I lost my train of thought."

Miss Fromme glared at Robby Zao who was laughing in his seat.

"Mr. Zao," Miss Fromme said firmly. "Is your writer's journal opened and ready? Or do you want extra homework?" Then The General turned to me. "Brian, please take your seat and see me after lunch."

"Miss Fromme?" Josh Mendez said in a whisper, as he barely raised his hand. "I'm supposed to go to the nurse's office and take my antibiotic now. I had strep throat all weekend."

Miss Fromme did not look happy. Thanks to my undone but soon-to-be, I'm sure, finished sloppy copy and a school fire drill, Miss Fromme's morning class time was quickly slipping away. She took the note from Josh's mother.

"Brian," Miss Fromme said. "Please accompany Josh to the nurse."

"But, Miss Fromme," I said. I held out my hands. I couldn't believe I was actually speaking. "I was just about to include some very important and descriptive information about the neighborhood-famous Harry Harrington."

Miss Fromme put both hands on her hips. "That won't be necessary, Brian," she said. "Class, let's get to our journals."

On the way to the nurse, Josh jiggled my sleeve. "You can tell me about Harry Harrington," he said. "I hate taking medicine. I need the distraction."

"Well," I said, "Harry Harrington is not

only neighborhood-famous because of his amazing guitar playing but also because of his two beautiful older sisters."

"I saw them once in a car," said Josh.

I nodded my head. "Harry told my mother that his parents paid more attention to his sisters than they ever did to him. He said it made him feel about as worthwhile as a flea."

"I had lice once," Josh said as he scratched his head.

"Fleas are different," I told him. "Fleas are something that my mother seems to have a soft touch for. She told Harry Harrington that he was more than welcome to 'come by the house anytime.' Harry took my mother at her word and started showing up for dinner nearly every single day. Once he even cooked us his recipe for chicken à la mode. Which, by the way, was not half bad."

"Chicken à la mode?" said Josh. He rubbed his belly. "I never heard of that before. But I wish I had some now."

We made a turn past the "Who's Who in School" bulletin board. Ana's face was plastered alongside the poem she wrote on leaves.

LEAVES
by Ana Newburg   Miss Fromme

Falling, falling from the trees,
Gold and red and orange leaves.
Children jump in raked-up piles,
Dogs come sniffing with a smile.
Squirrels take some for their nest.
I like autumn. It's the best.

"Anyway," I went on. I shrugged off the poem. "It was so annoying having Harry Harrington around my house all the time. When I wanted to use the video game, he was already playing it. If I called my mother to tell her I'd be late or something, Harry Harrington would answer the phone. 'Higman residence,' he'd say as if he actually lived there."

Josh shook his head. "A flea," he said. "They're hard to get rid of."

"Exactly." I nodded. I was glad he was listening. "But then bad news turned into good news. Denny lent me his old acoustic guitar when I told him I wanted to learn. And now he and Harry both take the time to teach me chords. G, C, D, A."

I showed Josh the tips of my fingers. "I'm already getting calluses," I said. "That shows I'm really practicing."

Josh and I walked into the nurse's office. Mrs. Dunn checked Josh's name off a list, then opened the door of the small refrigerator she kept next to one of the sickbeds. I positioned myself for a little rest.

"Don't lie on that," Mrs. Dunn told me.

"I'm planning on getting sick later," I told her. "Maybe I should just stay now."

My mind was swirling with so much stuff. I began to wish that I had a piece of paper with me. I had this urge to write it all down. That's when I knew I was really not well.

Mrs. Dunn filled a teaspoon with gross pink stuff. "This is the part I hate," Josh said. "Quick, tell me the rest." But Josh swallowed his medicine so fast there wasn't even time for a joke. Okay, so maybe now Josh was feeling a little bit better, but as soon as we left the nurse's office to walk back down the hall, I began to feel sick all over.

Chapter Five
Raining Cats and Dogs

In my head, I wrote The Franklin *horoscope tip:*

Caution! Planets are crisscrossing. This is NOT your lucky day.

I squeaked my sneakers down the hall. "I'm really in trouble," I said to Josh.

"No kidding," he said. "Wait until you get home."

Josh wiped a pink smudge onto his sleeve. "But getting back to that howling noise. The one you were telling us about in class. . . ."

The howling noise?

"Oh, right," I said. "You mean the *hoow-wooooow* that was coming from somewhere?"

"Yep," said Josh.

Then just like that, the soggy, rainy, wet morning came back to me as if it were only yesterday. . . .

"I left my plane drawings on the floor and got up from the couch to investigate the howling noise. I was just about to check inside one of the hall closets, when Stevie made one of his so-called beeline dashes from under the table and yanked the front door open.

" 'It's a dog,' said Stevie, bending over and practically dragging it into the house.

" 'How did he get here?' I wondered out loud.

" 'It's raining cats and dogs outside,' Stevie said. 'That's how he got here.'

" 'Raining cats and dogs,' my mother repeated over and over as she dried the mutt with a bathroom towel.

" 'That sounds like a newspaper headline,' said Pop.

" 'Look at his spots,' I said. 'They look like black and brown patches.'

" 'That's his name,' said Stevie. 'Patches.'

" 'It can't be his name,' I said. 'It's not our dog.'

" 'I'll run an ad,' Pop said. 'LOST DOG FOUND. WHITE WITH BROWN AND BLACK SPOTS.'

" 'Patches,' said Stevie.

" 'Right,' said Pop. 'And if no one turns up, we'll say he's ours and call it a day. Now how about some lunch?'

"Anyway, after running the ad for a couple of weeks, no one showed up, and that's how Patches arrived."

"Ha! Ha!" Josh laughed as we opened the classroom door. "That was a funny story."

Miss Fromme turned to look at us. She sipped some water.

"Okay, boys, now take your seats. We're on page thirty-eight in our math books," she said.

Nadine Ali raised her hand. The tiny gold bells on her bracelet jingled.

"Miss Fromme," she said. "I was just wondering about one little part in Brian's story. Was the *hooooow-wow* howling coming from a ghost or the wind?"

"It was a dog," said Josh. "That's how they ended up taking their dog, Patches, in and keeping her."

I folded my arms. So did Miss Fromme.

I had a quick flashback. I remembered Denny staring hard into my face like a comrade preparing me for battle.

"And if The General folds her arms, it means she's ready for war," he said.

"It seems like you have a captive audience," Miss Fromme said to me. She closed her pencil on page 38 and looked at her watch for the millionth time. "You have two minutes to finish."

I stood up straight. I thought about my options. Go into battle, or go home with a zero.

"Well," I began. I started to remember. **"It was Saturday. . . .**

"I slowly inched out of my bedroom, leaving Stevie and Patches to whatever sweet dreams a boy and a dog could have. I didn't want to wake them up. I was on a mission and it was a secret.

"I was about to dig up the peanut butter jar that I had buried in the backyard near my pop's garage. The peanut butter jar had all

the money I needed in it to buy the guitar I wanted.

"I shoveled out the jar with one of my mother's gardening tools and brushed off the dirt. I held up the jar to look inside. Everything was still in there. I walked up the back porch steps and smelled coffee already brewing from the kitchen. Pop was up and reading the Saturday morning edition of the newspaper.

" 'Got plans?' he asked, looking over his paper. He dripped a teaspoon of honey onto his toast and paid close attention to the peanut butter jar I was holding in my hand.

" 'See this?' I said. I unscrewed the top and took out the sock that I had stuffed with money. Actually, there were two socks. One sock had the money. The other sock had more socks stuffed inside. That was my decoy. Just in case anybody ever found the jar and tried to steal it.

"Pop watched me pour about a pound of cornflakes into an ice-cream bowl. He looked at the crumbs of dirt that circled the jar around the table.

" 'Yep,' he said. 'I see it.'

"I held up the sock. 'I saved enough money in here to get myself an electric guitar. Denny said I could borrow his amplifier whenever he wasn't using it. I'm starting a band.'

"I could see right away that Pop was impressed.

" 'I admire a boy with gumption,' he said.

"Translation: a kid like me who could take it upon himself to have the courage to do something *outstanding*.

40

"All of a sudden I began to hear a stirring at the top of the stairs. The house was waking up. Steps padded closer to the landing. Milk dribbled down my chin. A flurry of paws clicked their way toward the back steps leading into the kitchen. It was Patches. That meant that Stevie was not far behind. I imagined my brother wide-awake and full of so-called entertainment.

" 'Peanut sat on a railroad track. . . . Toot! Toot! Peanut butter!'

"Oh no! Pretty soon my mother would be asking, 'Brian, honey, I need your help to keep an eye on Stevie while I give a piano lesson.'

"No way! I didn't want to take Stevie with me while I picked up my new guitar. This was going to be a moment in time that I wanted to remember forever! In a good way, I mean.

" 'Got to go, Pop,' I said in a rush.

" 'What's your hurry?' Pop asked me. 'How about some company?'

"I grabbed my sock and gave him a hug. Me and

Pop. Wow! What a morning! What could be better than that?"

Miss Fromme took a deep breath. "Two minutes are up," she said.

"Phew." I waved my hand like a fan in my face. "It's getting hot in here."

Ana tilted her head to one side and sat back like Miss Fromme.

"Can we hear the rest?" Robby asked, turning his seat toward the white board. "It sounds like something's going to happen."

"Something *is* going to happen," I told Miss Fromme. I slinked back to my chair. "It's not an excuse. It's a reason with gumption."

A reason with gumption, I thought to myself. I'll have to write that down in my journal. Maybe I should start a vocabulary section in *The Franklin*.

STEW: To cook by boiling slowly: To worry, as in to stew in one's own juices.

That was me. I was slowly boiling, and Miss Fromme looked like she was just about to raise the heat. She got up from her chair, pushed in her seat, and began to walk toward my desk.

Chapter Six
Fried to a Crisp

If I ever write an entertainment section for The Franklin, *I might not include a crossword puzzle. I do not like fitting words into boxes that meet across and down with a joining letter in between.*

I am more the word-jumble type. The word I am thinking of now is:

LEHP!

I watched Miss Fromme slowly making her way toward me. All of a sudden the loudspeaker crackled.

"Please excuse the *outstanding* interruption," Mrs. Confrontini, the school secretary, said. "Will the *outstanding* Brian Higman please report to the office."

Oh no. I wasn't even in trouble yet and I was already in trouble.

I looked at Ana. Even she looked nervous.

Miss Fromme leaned over to open the window. "Robby, please accompany Brian to the office," she said without even looking.

Out in the hallway Robby said, "Whoa! Are you just lucky, Big Hig? Or are you really in trouble?"

"I don't know," I said to Robby. "But I'm going to find out soon."

"Speaking of finding out," said Robby. "Are we starting the band or not? Did you get the guitar? What's going on?"

It was a good question. But it was not a question that I was ready to answer. I was still thinking about me and Pop on Saturday morning as we walked toward Myers's Music.

"It was just like one of those mornings you'd see in the movies," I told Robby, even though he didn't ask. **"The sun was out, the sky was blue, and the birds were singing a tune. . . .**

"I liked spending time with Pop alone. It was a rare occasion when Pop had a Saturday off from work. Being a salesperson was not an easy job. Especially on Saturdays. Pop said it was like the whole world was out buying refrigerators and ovens on Saturdays.

"We crossed the street and I hummed a little tune. Me and Pop on our way to the music store. That was something to sing about. But just as we turned onto Station Avenue, I looked down the block and saw someone familiar. It was Harry Harrington. Where was *he* going at this time of day? He was coming our way. He was heading toward Myers's Music. . . ."

There was a brown paper bag on Mrs. Confrontini's desk. It had my name written on it with crayon. It was my lunch.

"Hello, Brian," Mrs. Confrontini said. "It's

nice to see you again. Your mother dropped this by for you."

I tried to smile for Mrs. Confrontini.

"And by the way," she said, "I finally had the chance to meet that little brother of yours. The one that you were looking for the other day? I hear he'll be coming to school next year."

"Was he wearing two hats?" I asked.

Mrs. Confrontini laughed. "Yes, he was," she said.

I knew it. Stevie had stood in front of Mrs.

Confrontini's desk still wearing the raccoon cap with the earflaps snapped and the sailor hat on top.

"Since when does your brother wear two hats?" Robby asked me on our way back to class.

"Since two days ago," I said.

Miss Fromme glanced over and waved us in.

I crumpled my lunch bag inside my desk, opened my book, and got to work. Who cared about a zero anyway?

I'd start a "Manners" page for *The Franklin* and settle things once and for all.

Dear Manners Matter,

Do you think it is bad manners for a teacher to fail an unfortunate yet <u>outstanding</u> student without listening to his whole reason first?

Yours truly,
A Really Nice Kid

Dear A Really Nice Kid,

It would be very bad manners, indeed.

Sincerely,
Manners Matter

Kids all over the world would thank me.

I raised my hand. Miss Fromme shook her head. There would be no more interruptions for the rest of the morning.

We went through a lesson on identifying clouds. Cumulus clouds were puffy and piled up. Stratus clouds could be flat or layered or both. Cirrus clouds were curly.

We also had the pleasure of taking a pop math quiz on two- and three-digit division.

It was nearly lunchtime by the time Miss Fromme looked up and said, "Somehow, we have gotten through everything. Brian, I am still interested in hearing how your story ends."

What's this? I thought. The General is giving me another chance? The rest of my life could still be saved.

"You were telling us something about a guitar?" Miss Fromme said.

"You missed a lot," Robby Zao informed everyone. "Big Hig and his pop were just about to buy the guitar he saved up for when the neighborhood-famous Harry Harrington showed up at the same time."

Miss Fromme lifted her eyebrows and smiled like she was worried. "Go ahead, Brian," she said.

Me, Pop, and Harry stopped right in front of the music store.

" 'What are you doing here?' I said to Harry.

"Harry smiled and shook hands with Pop. Harry's flannel shirt hung loose around his shoulders. I wanted a shirt like that.

" 'I was just on my way to your house,' said Harry.

" 'A likely story,' I said to myself.

"I reached into the pocket of my jeans and took out the blue-speckled Fender pick that Denny had given me. It was a medium.

Denny told me, 'A good guitar player is always ready to play.' That was me. And in about five minutes I'd have the guitar to go with it.

" 'Morning, George,' Mr. Myers said to my pop. 'Morning, fellows,' he said to us. Mr. Myers bobbed his head from side to side like a toy on the dashboard of a car.

" 'Where's that little brother of yours?' Mr. Myers asked me. He chuckled and gave Pop a wink.

"Pop stood smiling with his hands folded and his head shaking. He looked like he was praying for Stevie and understanding Mr. Myers at the same time.

" 'That little guy is really something,' Mr. Myers said, as he unlocked the front door. 'Just give me a minute inside.'

"We all waited while Mr. Myers got settled.

"I looked at Harry. He wasn't talking and neither was I.

"I cupped my hands around my face and pressed my nose against the window. There it was. The red-and-black Stratocaster. A glimmer of sun hit it just right, and it shined like a million bucks.

"Mr. Myers was taking his sweet ol' time.

He was turning on the lights, turning back the CLOSED sign to OPEN.

" 'Come on, come on,' I said to myself. I kept my sneaker close to the door, so I'd be the first one inside.

" 'Brian's here to buy a guitar,' Pop said all of a sudden to Harry.

"Harry shuffled a few pieces of gravel to one side.

" 'Want some help picking it out?' he asked me.

" 'No thanks,' I said just like that. 'I've got my guitar all picked out, and I have the money right here.'

"That's when I pulled out my sock. Only when I pulled out my sock, another sock fell out, and another and another.

"I had taken the decoy by mistake! My dreams were ruined.

" 'I have to go home,' I said to Pop. 'I'll be right back.'

"I took off running like an Olympic racer, darting around people and jumping curbs. 'See you,' said Harry as he gave me a wave. And when I turned the corner I saw him walk into Myers's Music."

The lunch bell rang and nobody moved. Well, nobody except me. I was starving after a morning like this.

"What a flea!" Josh mumbled.

"Brian," Miss Fromme said, "I have been very patient with you this morning. I think you will agree to that. But the fact of the matter remains. You do not have your written assignment. Please see me after lunch."

I could feel my eyes beginning to glaze.

"Does this mean I'm getting a zero?" I asked. I might as well know now before I tried to eat anything. The sloppy copy loomed in the distance like a threatening weather report.

WiLL the Hurricane Hit?
the Franklin reported.
Stay tuned for more
DISaSTrous NEWS.

"After lunch, Mr. Higman," Miss Fromme said firmly. Then she pointed the way toward the cafeteria as if I might have forgotten.

Chapter Seven
The Missing Sock

→WANTED DEAD OR ALIVE ←
Brian Higman
Alias: BIG HIG
REWARD

"You're in deep trouble now," Ana said to me in the cafeteria as she walked past my table with her lunch tray and sat down right behind us. "You can't fool Miss Fromme with that story of yours."

"I don't mess with the facts," I said, reciting Pop's favorite motto.

Robby Zao ripped open his vegetarian wrap.

"She's right," Josh said. "Miss Fromme will never believe you."

I was about to take a bite of my ham and cheese when I noticed a pink piece of paper inside my sandwich. I pulled it out. It was a note from my mother.

Hi Honey ♡
Family meeting after school! Try not to be late. Stevie has a surprise. Love,
xox Mom

I wiped the mustard off it and stuck it into my pocket.

"Why does your mother leave notes in your sandwich?" Josh asked me.

"My mother is not normal," I said.

Nadine Ali opened her chips. "I think your mother is fun," she said. "Remember the time we had a cookout in your backyard and it started to rain?"

Ana was listening. She pointed a carrot

stick toward our table. "I was at that cookout," she said.

"Ha! Ha!" Robby laughed. "We all got stuck eating soggy hot dogs and hamburgers inside your garage when the backyard drain clogged up."

"Remember?" said Josh. "And the backyard puddle got bigger and bigger until the tips of our sneakers were wet?"

I pictured the moment in my head. Me with my baked beans rolling off the side of my plate as we all pushed further inside the garage. We watched as my mother shuffled dinner plates onto this huge puddle like a deck of cards, while the rain cleaned the dishes for her.

"I think it was a good idea," said Nadine.

"I agree," said Ana.

In front of the cafeteria, Mrs. Wagner, the P.E. teacher, turned up the volume on Beethoven's Fifth Symphony. This was her signal for us to begin cleaning up our trays.

I, Big Hig, personally did not mind when Mrs. Wagner played her weekly tunes of classical music. Every week she had a new theme. All the composers had weird names. Last week it was Bach. The week before that it was Vivaldi.

Mrs. Wagner told us she got the idea from a circus trainer who tamed wild beasts.

"Okay, *outstanding* students," Mrs. Wagner said. "Let's get ready to go outside."

In the school yard, the kids from Miss Fromme's class were starting to crowd around me.

"Did you get the guitar?" asked Tyrone.

"What happened?" Chris C. wanted to know.

"I think Harry bought it," Jacelle said. Ana and Nadine and Martin Adaji moved closer to me like ants to a crumb.

I clawed my fingers through the chain-link fence. I was as angry as a wet hen just thinking about it.

"It was all downhill from there!"

"I left Pop at the music store, ran home, sprung the back door open, looked on the kitchen table, and saw that my sock was gone. The peanut butter jar was right where I had left it. So was the ice-cream bowl with half a pound of cereal still inside.

" 'Where's my money?' I shouted.

"I checked underneath the table to see if Stevie was playing 'bank.' He wasn't.

" 'Anybody home?' I yelled. No answer. Not even Patches came running.

" 'Looks like the troops have gone,' said Pop. The screen door closed behind him.

" 'Pop!' I said. 'My money is gone.'

"Pop rested his thumbs inside his pockets. I was glad he had followed me home. 'That money's got to be here somewhere,' he said.

"I rushed upstairs to check out Stevie's so-called hiding places, while Pop searched the whole downstairs. I looked inside the spaghetti pot that Stevie kept under a blanket. I crammed my way through his secret shoe pile. I scavenged through his hat collection. No luck.

" 'Any luck?' I called out to Pop.

" 'Not yet,' he said. 'Check with Denny.'

"I squeaked the door open to Denny's room.

" 'Denny! Denny!' I tapped his pillow. 'My money is gone. My sock is missing. It was on the kitchen table. Did you see it?'

"Denny rolled over and squinted his eyes.

" 'What time is it?' asked Denny.

" 'Great, just great,' I said to myself as I closed the door to Denny's room. Denny didn't know where my money was. He didn't even know it was nearly noon.

"I went downstairs and found Pop in the kitchen.

" 'It's not upstairs,' I said to Pop. 'I looked all over. It's gone.'

"Just then, Pop pitched his thumb toward a pink note on the refrigerator:

Went to library.
Stevie and Patches
with me.
Love,
mom xox

"Pop opened the kitchen cabinet and grabbed two granola bars.

" 'Come on,' he said. 'Let's go.'

Mrs. Wagner blew the school-yard whistle. "All *outstanding* boys and girls please line up for class," she bellowed through the megaphone.

"What happened next, Big Hig?" Josh asked.

"No talking, please," Mrs. Wagner said.

Josh shrugged his shoulders and lined up with the rest of the *outstanding* students of Franklin Elementary. At least my mother had packed me an *outstanding* lunch. I needed the strength. After all, I was just about to come face-to-face once again with the *outstanding* General Fromme.

Now HEAR THIS!
REPORT TO BATTLE STATIONS!
THE SHIP IS GOING DOWN!

Chapter Eight
An Illuminating Mess

Outstanding Joke:

Question: Why did the centipede
cross the road?
Answer: To get to the other side.

I was not in a funny or original mood.

When we settled back into the classroom, Josh Mendez asked an *outstanding* question.

"Miss Fromme, isn't Brian's story like a *verbal* sloppy copy?"

If I would have had braces, you would have been able to see them flashing a smile in the afternoon sun. Josh was right! I meant to give Miss Fromme a *verbal* sloppy copy all along! It was an experiment.

Miss Fromme thought about it for a moment.

"You could say that, Josh," Miss Fromme said.

Could this be true? Was Miss Fromme actually going to set me free and believe my bonafide story? A rush of relief swept over me. I was no longer a captive! Blue skies were on their way.

Suddenly Miss Fromme arched her eyebrows. You could even say that she looked kind of sorry for what she was about to say next.

"However," said Miss Fromme. "That was not the assignment. The assignment was a *written* sloppy copy, and in all fairness to everyone, Brian did not do that."

"But his money was stolen!" said Fareed.

"He was just about to go and get Stevie," Joelle hollered.

"Harry Harrington, that flea!" said Zachary.

"Excuse me," Miss Fromme said. "But would this entire class like to stay in for recess tomorrow? Brian, may I see you for a moment?"

I buried my head in my hands. I felt the comfort of what an ostrich must feel like when it hides its head in the sand.

There was a knock on the classroom door. I looked up. It was our principal, Mr. Zifferman.

"Good afternoon, Miss Fromme," Mr. Zifferman said. "Good afternoon, *outstanding* students."

He lifted his shoulders and squeezed his eyes like a baby who just got tickled.

"I would like to introduce you to our new student teacher, Mr. Minty. Mr. Minty comes to Franklin Elementary fresh from State University," Mr. Zifferman said.

"*. . . Freddy, the Freshman, the freshest kid in town . . .*"

Oh no! One of Stevie's so-called entertainment songs was stuck inside my brain.

"Do you mind if we stay and observe for a while?" Mr. Zifferman asked.

"Not at all," said Miss Fromme. "Brian Higman was just about to finish a story."

"Is that right, Brian?" asked Mr. Minty.

"I'm kind of at the end," I said, hoping to change the *outstanding* Mr. Minty's mind.

All of a sudden I understood the difference between my life and the life of an ostrich. An ostrich would never have to speak in front of a principal or a new student teacher. I sideswiped a look at Robby Zao. He was shaking his head up and down like a bird that was trying to talk.

"That's all right," Mr. Zifferman told me. "Just make believe we're not even here."

I raised my eyes. I had to do it.

"Well," I said without even blinking. **"I was just about to go to the library with my pop to see if my mother knew where my missing sock with the money was."**

Miss Fromme cleared her throat.

"Go on," said Mr. Zifferman.

"I had a sneaky suspicion that my little brother, Stevie, could be at the bottom of the missing money.

"When I got to the library, Patches was tied to the bench outside. He wagged his tail when he saw me coming.

" 'Good boy, Patches,' I said. And I gave him a pat.

"Inside, Stevie had made himself perfectly comfortable on the floor of the young-readers' section. He was taking the leftover clothespins that Mrs. Saha, the librarian, hadn't used to hang up her decorations and was attaching them to his shirt.

"'Look! I'm a porcupine,' Stevie said, standing up when he saw me.

"The clothespins were sticking out in crazy directions.

"'Stevie,' I said. 'I have something really important to ask you.'

"By now my face was covered in sweat. I was panting.

"'What's wrong?' my mother asked. She brushed my hair back with her hand.

"'Mom!' I said. 'Did you see my sock? I left it on the table. It had my money inside. I was going to buy my guitar this morning, but somebody took my money.'

"'You're going to buy a guitar?' asked my mother.

"'I saw the sock,' said Stevie.

"I turned around. 'I knew it!' I yelled.

"Stevie saw the look on my face. It was the same look that I had the time he took my favorite shirt and used it to dress up a snowman.

"That's when Stevie threw his sailor hat on the floor and made one of his so-called beeline dashes, crashing his way past Mrs. Saha and charging out the door.

" 'Better go after him,' Pop told me.

" 'And come right back,' said my mother."

I stopped talking. It felt like a good time to take a break.

"Thank you, Brian," Mr. Zifferman said. "Later on, you can stop by my office and tell me the rest."

Miss Fromme cheerfully showed them both to the door.

I let out a breath that could have blown any stratus, cirrus, or cumulus clouds straight across the sky.

Josh Mendez raised his hand.

"No more questions," Miss Fromme said.

"But Stevie ran away," I said. "I tried to catch him, but I'm not a fast runner."

I sat back down as soon as I said it. I had crossed the war line. General Fromme did not like calling out. Ana Newburg raised her hand.

"Miss Fromme," she said. "Brian's story gave me a connection."

A connection? I thought. Wasn't that another one of Miss Fromme's famous mottos for writing? Make the connections whenever you can.

"When Brian told us about his little brother, it reminded me of my little sister, Bella," said Ana. "Every time we bring Bella to the supermarket, she takes cans off the shelves and puts them in our wagon. I could write a story about that."

Wait a minute. Was Ana trying to help me? I gave her a smile just in case she was. And then I took another chance.

"My brother was lost," I said to Miss Fromme. My arms began to wave and spin like a carnival entertainer. "We couldn't find him anywhere."

Miss Fromme was not smiling.

Her face looked flushed. She smacked down her book.

The battlefield is getting smaller. Enemy tanks are moving in. We need more troops! Quick! To the foxhole!

"It's practically the end," I said without thinking. I was wishing I had a white flag to wave.

"It *is* the end," Miss Fromme said. Her patience was gone. Her limit had been tested. "You will not be taking up any more of my class time," she said. "See me after school, Mr. Higman."

The ruling was in. I, Big Hig, would not be seeing the light of day for a good solid week. But that didn't seem to bother Miss Fromme. She went right on with her lessons.

"Writers' journals open and ready," Miss Fromme said for the second time today. "Kayla, what did you write about yesterday? And how did you illuminate the moment?"

"I wrote about the expression on my grandmother's face as my mother lit the candles on her birthday cake," she said.

"Very nice," Miss Fromme said. "How about you, Martin?"

Martin Adaji pointed his finger. "I saw a squirrel. His tail was fluffy and bent like a comma. That's all I wrote," said Martin.

"Good simile," said

Miss Fromme. "Boys and girls, you have twenty minutes to illuminate a moment. If you can't think of anything, look inside your journals for your seed ideas. Ready? Begin."

Miss Fromme set the timer and we all got to work.

I spiraled to a clean page and found my pencil. Before I wrote, I pictured the whole thing in my mind.

I left the library running after Stevie, following his trail of clothespins. "Hoooooow woooow," Patches was howling near the library bench.

"You can't leave that dog here," Mrs. Saha said. "He'll upset the whole neighborhood."

"Take Patches with you," my mother called after me. "And come right back with Stevie."

I looked for Stevie down the block.

"There he is," I shouted to Pop. "I'll get him."

It wasn't hard to see my brother. Stevie was the only kid running down the block wearing a raccoon hat with clothespins falling off him. He made a quick getaway into somebody's backyard.

Where was he going? I got to the driveway and stopped.

"Hello, Brian," Mrs. Confrontini said. "Are you enjoying your weekend so far?"

Mrs. Confrontini, the school secretary, was watering the flowers on her porch. I never even knew she lived there. "Hello," I said. Not sure what to say next.

Patches sniffed the edge of her lawn.

I scribbled down what happened next.

"Are you looking for something?" Mrs. Confrontini asked me.

Mrs. Confrontini did not have radar. My feet were stepping from side to side. My shirt was hanging out of my pants and one of my sneakers was untied.

"I'm looking for my little brother," I said. "You haven't met him yet."

This was before she had the pleasure of meeting Stevie today when he brought my lunch to school with my mother.

"What does he look like?" asked Mrs. Confrontini.

I shook my head at what I was about to say.

"He's about this big," I said, holding my hand up to here.

"Yes?" said Mrs. Confrontini.

"And he has on a raccoon hat with earflaps that snap underneath," I said.

"Yes," said Mrs. Confrontini.

"...And clothespins sticking out of his shirt."

Mrs. Confrontini tapped her watering can. "I did see a boy who looked like that," she said. "I think he went in there."

Riiiiiiiiing! The buzzer went off on Miss Fromme's desk.

"Time's up," she said. She clicked off the timer.

And the rest of the day was a blank.

When the three o'clock bell rang, I was startled out of my social studies book. "Ponce de León," I said as Miss Fromme mentioned something about discovering Florida.

The class stood up and began to gather their books and backpacks and jackets from the hall closet. Some of them made sure they had copied down their homework assignment for tomorrow. Others, like me, simply slid their social studies books into their desks and waited to see Miss Fromme. Josh and Robby huddled around.

"We're still starting the band, right, Big Hig?" Robby asked me.

"It's just a matter of time," I said.

Miss Fromme began to erase the board.

"Good luck," said Josh. "Things can't get much worse."

I rubbed my head. "You wish," I said. It was the story of my life.

Chapter Nine
The Last Chance

EXTRA!
Brian Higman sets universal record for most detentions in world history.

When the classroom was empty, Miss Fromme made some space on her desk. She pushed aside some books and folders and papers and then waited for me to step forward.

"I'm really sorry, Miss Fromme," I said.

I kicked the leg on her desk by mistake.

"You had a busy weekend, Brian," Miss Fromme said. She almost sounded nice.

I tried to remember what Denny had told me to do if Miss Fromme ever sounded nice. I scoured my brain. He never said anything. I was on my own.

caution: ALL transmitters are about to BLOW. THIS IS NOT A TEST.

"Miss Fromme," I said. "I'm not trying to fool you. Everything I told you is true."

Miss Fromme opened her top desk drawer. She took out a box of crackers and placed three on a napkin for me.

"Here," she said. Then she pushed up her chair. "Why don't you tell me the rest."

"I looked for Stevie all over Mrs. Confrontini's yard. I looked behind the concrete birdbath and inside the garden shed. I looked under some bushes and got little green pieces of fern stuck in my hair. But I couldn't find him.

"Patches began to pull on his leash and bark in a different direction. He must have picked up Stevie's scent.

"'Good boy, Patches,' I said, letting him take the lead.

"Patches led me three houses down from

Mrs. Confrontini's house right to where Harry Harrington lived. That's when I saw Stevie.

"He was sitting on the front steps with Harry's two beautiful older sisters. One beautiful sister was helping Stevie untangle a couple of twigs that got twisted in his T-shirt. The other beautiful sister was straightening out his raccoon hat. I had never exactly met Harry Harrington's two beautiful older sisters. And this did not seem like the best time to introduce myself.

"'He's so cute,' the first beautiful sister said to me. 'Is he your brother?'

"'We're thinking of keeping him,' the other beautiful sister said.

"I was just about to say, 'Take him,' when I realized they might want to trade in Harry for Stevie.

"'He's mine,' I said, raising my voice.

"Stevie got up. He bent his knees and jumped off the porch.

"'Geronimo!' Stevie yelled. 'You'll never catch me while I'm still alive!'

"What was my mother teaching him at home? I rushed a quick good-bye to the sisters and took off after my brother.

"I held on to Patches's leash as we chased Stevie home.

"Denny's band was already rehearsing. The bass kick on the drum thumped like a heartbeat from inside my house. I could hear my brother's voice singing deep and low. Harry Harrington wailed out two lead notes.

"I stopped dead. The band was rehearsing. Harry was back from Myers's Music. Did he buy my guitar? I had to see. I pushed the basement window open. I couldn't tell. I stretched my neck. I thought I saw it.

" 'Hooooow wooooow!' Patches pulled away from the leash and began to bark up the maple tree.

" 'Stevie,' I mumbled. I ran to the tree and shook my fist.

" 'Where is my money?' I yelled to him.

"My brother had climbed up the maple again. There he was curled up on a branch. Stevie threw some leaves on my head.

" 'I'm not coming down,' he told me.

Miss Fromme stopped me right at the good part. I waited for the final blow.

"First of all," Miss Fromme said. "I can tell

you right now that this will never happen again."

"Never, Miss Fromme," I said.

"And second of all," Miss Fromme went on. "I would like to tell you, Brian, that everything you told the class this morning *and* this afternoon is exactly the kind of story that you could be writing down on paper."

I knew it had been a long day for me, but that didn't make any sense.

"Brian," she said. And she patted her desk. "I want you to write down the rest of your story."

"You mean I'm getting a second chance?"

"Write like you're talking to me," said Miss Fromme. "Remember, this is your sloppy copy."

I took out a blank piece of paper. I wanted to get this off my chest. I also had to get home for the family meeting.

Brian Higman   Miss Fromme

I was frantically shaking my fist up a tree when Ace Randall, the bass player in Questions No Answers, asked, "What are you doing?"

Her long brown hair was dyed blue on one side. She flipped it back.

"Stevie's up there," I said.

My brother Denny had stepped outside the basement and stood around the tree with the rest of the band.

Denny looked up. Stevie threw more leaves.

"Is this about your sock?" Denny asked me, brushing leaves off his shirt.

"It doesn't matter anymore," I said. "Harry already bought the guitar."

Harry Harrington made a face.

"Dude," said Harry. "Your pop saved the day. No way was I going to get into a family argument and buy that Stratocaster. He said that guitar was already yours."

In one fat second I loved my pop more than anything else in the world.

I didn't feel so bad about Harry either.

When my parents came back from the library, Pop got Stevie out of the tree.

"That was a plumb dandy mess you got yourself into," Pop told Stevie as he edged him down a ladder.

Stevie ran into my mother's arms. "Flo!" he cried. "I was stuck."

In the kitchen my parents sat us all down at the table.

"One of you will be punished," Pop said. "Which one will it be?"

All I could think of was, Great, punish Stevie. If it wasn't for him none of this would've happened. I would've already had my guitar. I would've had my homework done. I wouldn't be in this stupid kitchen. It was all Stevie's fault.

Stevie was sitting on the kitchen chair. His feet didn't even touch the floor.

"Punish me," I said to Pop. "I was the one who was supposed to bring him back to the library. I'm sorry I lost my temper."

Pop squinted an eye at me and patted my back.

"That's right, Brian," Pop said. "Bringing back Stevie was your responsibility. And just for recognizing that fact, you will not be punished this time. Sometimes a person can learn his lesson by having the gumption to admit it."

"Wow, thanks," I said. And I hugged him tight. I even gave Stevie a little rub, though I washed my hands right after.

Mom held the peanut butter jar in her hand. "Let's get this straight once and for all," my mother said. I looked up at the ceiling my mother was about to hit.

"Stevie, did you take Brian's sock?" she asked.

My little brother was sniffling into a napkin.

"No," said Stevie. "I didn't."

"It just didn't disappear," said my mother.

Pop took out his wallet and gave me twenty dollars. "In the meantime," he said, "how about we take a walk back to Myers's Music and put down a deposit on that guitar before anybody else decides to buy it."

My pop was a genius.

"I'm finished, Miss Fromme." I handed Miss Fromme my sloppy copy. I looked in my notebook to double-check that I had written down all my homework assignments.

"Thank you, Brian," said Miss Fromme. "I'll look forward to reading it."

RAH! RAH! The Loser ties in OVERTIME!

"And, Brian," Miss Fromme called as I was nearly free out the door. "There will be no more chances."

Chapter Ten
The Outstanding and Exuberant Brian Higman

I walked home from school in a fog. The sloppy copy was done. That was a load off my mind. But I still had the weight of the missing money on my brain.

When I finally arrived home from school, I opened the door to find everyone waiting for me in the living room for the family meeting. My mother was sitting on her piano bench with Stevie and Patches nearby.

Stevie was wearing only one hat this afternoon. It was the sailor hat. He was also wearing a pair of blue mittens with one of my mother's aprons tied around his neck like a cape. Pop and Denny were sitting on the couch alongside Harry Harrington and Darleen and Cynthia, Harry's two beautiful sisters.

"What's going on?" I asked. I dumped my backpack on the rug.

Stevie held out his arms like a game-show host.

"Hooow! Wow!" Stevie said. He crawled on his hands and knees with his mittens. *"Ruff! Ruff!"* Stevie panted and sniffed around.

Patches wagged his tail.

"When does it end?" I asked my mother.

Stevie kept barking and acting like a dog. He shook his head. He licked at the air. He pretended to dig for a bone under the rug.

"Ta! Da!" said Stevie as he clapped his mittens and pulled out the missing sock!

"My sock!" I said. "I can't believe it." I pulled it away, and Patches jumped up. He tried to wrestle the sock from my hand.

"He's the robber!" Stevie yelled, pointing a mitten at Patches. Then Stevie took a so-called flying leap off two pillows and yanked the sock from his paws.

So that was it? The mystery was solved.

I took my seat at the family meeting and listened to the story from Stevie.

It seemed that today, while I was in class,

Stevie had gone into the backyard to look for worms. Spying on worms was one of Stevie's so-called science experiments. While he was carefully laying the slimy serpents back into the dirt, he noticed Patches sniffing around near Pop's garage. This was not unusual. Patches is a big sniffer. But then Patches began to dig something up.

Guess what it was! You guessed it. My sock. Patches had buried it and Stevie had caught him returning to the scene of the crime.

Well, I never would have suspected that a

dog could be a robber. I am not even sure if you can call a dog a robber. All I know is that Patches was the one who took it. Patches was the first one down the back kitchen steps the morning I left with Pop to buy my guitar. He must have smelled my sock. Liked it. Chewed it around. Then decided to keep it for himself.

What a dog!

The next morning I couldn't wait to get to school. I placed my peanut butter jar complete with money and sock on top of my desk where I knew it would be safe. Stevie would watch it for me.

I finished my cereal and put my bowl inside the dishwasher. I checked my backpack to make sure that I had all my homework.

My mother checked my forehead.

Stevie and Patches came shuffling down the stairs.

"Bye, Brian," Stevie said. I gave him a wave.

"See you later, Flo," I said to my mother as I whistled out the door.

Did I happen to mention that Ana Newburg was no longer my ex-best friend? I walked right up to her in the school yard this morning and said, "Ana, today I am going to buy my guitar.

"Fact number one," I said. "We think you'd make an outstanding bass player. Fact number two: We want to start a band with gumption. Fact number three: . . ."

Fact number three? The *gumption* threw me off.

"Big Hig doesn't mess with the facts," Robby told her.

"We're calling ourselves The Pitt," said Josh. "Since we'll be practicing in Big Hig's basement."

Ana rubbed the tips of her fingers. I'll bet she had calluses just like mine.

"Okay," said Ana. "I'll be in the band. But I'm not quitting the cello. And Nadine is still my friend."

Nadine Ali shook the charms on her bracelet. "Maybe I can play tambourine?" she asked.

My life was beginning to take a new turn.

I had an idea for a letter I would write to *The Franklin:*

Dear <u>Franklin Newsletter</u>,

   As a neighborhood reader, I would like to compliment you on your creative paper, <u>the Franklin Newsletter</u>, Someday, when I finally take over, and write my head off, I will tell you how it saved my life.

   It has been a pleasure doing business with you,

                    Yours truly,

                    Brian Higman

Mr. Zifferman was happy to see me. I was happy to see him.

It was my turn to be the loudspeaker announcer. I told him the rest of my story and then took a seat next to Mrs. Confrontini. When the Pledge of Allegiance was over, Mr. Zifferman handed me a piece of paper.

"All set?" he asked.

"All set," I said.

The loudspeaker crackled.

"The word of the day is *exuberant*," I read,

making sure that I did not hold my mouth too close to the microphone. "E-x-u-b-e-r-a-n-t. It is an adjective that means enthusiastic or lively. Today there will be no *exuberant* fire drills," I said. "We will be having *exuberant* chicken nuggets and an *exuberant* recess outside with the *exuberant* Mrs. Wagner after lunch."

Mrs. Confrontini turned off the switch.

"By the way," she said. "I'm glad that everything worked out with you and your missing sock. That story you were telling Mr. Zifferman sounded quite *exuberant*."

I was just about to tell Mrs. Confrontini that it was *not* a story, but then I realized it really was.

"It's historical nonfiction," I said.

In the classroom Miss Fromme handed back the sloppy copies from yesterday—including mine. Of course, there were a mess of suggestions and corrections, but I, Big Hig, did not really mind. I planned on keeping my five senses ready and alert for action. Sight, sound, smell, taste, and touch. My pad and pencil were in my top pocket. A true writer is always prepared to write. That was my new motto.

Chapter Eleven
A Happy Ending

After school, on the way back from Myers's Music, I carried my red-and-black Stratocaster in the new guitar case that Denny and Harry were able to get me for a bargain price. Even my pop had left work early to be a part of the *outstanding, exuberant,* and monumental occasion.

I guess you could say it was a family event.

My mother and Patches had showed up, too. Along with Darleen and Cynthia who held Stevie's hands while we were in the store.

"*Twinkle, twinkle, little guitar,*" Stevie sang.

"It's a beauty," Mr. Myers said. He counted out my money and tucked it into the register.

When I got home I played my guitar until it was time for supper. My mother whipped up my personal favorite—spaghetti and meat-balls.

"This is delicious," said Darleen.

"Mrs. Higman, may I have the recipe?" Cynthia asked.

Harry Harrington's two beautiful older sisters also said they'd be happy to stop by tomorrow to keep an eye on Stevie, if that was okay with my mother.

"Yes," I said. "That would be great. You're welcome to come by the house anytime."

As you can imagine, everybody went crazy when they heard about my guitar.

"You did it, Big Hig," said Robby Zao. "We're starting a band."

"Nice work, Hig," said Josh. He grabbed my hand and shook it.

The brand new day seemed destined to be bright.

Ana was the first one to put her homework into the homework bin on Miss Fromme's desk. Robby came back with Josh after accompanying him to the nurse. And Miss Fromme was standing in front of the white board, ready to set her timer.

"Okay, class," Miss Fromme said. "Fifteen minutes to write about a topic. Remember to visualize before you write and use your senses. Look through your journals for seed ideas if you need inspiration."

I flipped through my writer's notebook to see if I had any ideas.

Fishing trip with family . . . another zero . . . tomatoes are not only vegetables . . . a boy with gumption . . .

"Writers ready?"

"Miss Fromme," I said. I raised my hand.

I was just about to ask her if I could share a very descriptive and illuminated story about how our band, The Pitt, was going to enter the Franklin Elementary School Talent Show this spring.

But then I decided not to. Instead, I took out my sharpened pencil, smoothed open a clean page of paper, and wrote:

Brian Higman   Miss Fromme

   It all started yesterday when my little brother, Stevie, had a so-called idea....

Chapter Twelve
Big Hig's "FACTS" for Writing

» <u>Big Hig's "FACTS" for Writing</u> ←

1. Pay attention to the ordinary things that happen in your life and teach yourself to write them down.

2. Write about what you know OR research what you don't.

3. Organize your story with a beginning, a middle, and an end.

4. Think of the setting and the characters.

5. Visualize the scene in your head.

6. Choose outstanding and descriptive words.

7. Illuminate the moment including the five senses.

8. Don't be afraid to write with your voice.

9. Take a break if you get stuck.

10. DON'T GIVE UP !!!